DEAR
BUNNY...

Written by
Katie Cotton

Illustrated by
Blanca Gómez

Frances Lincoln
Children's Books

Dear Bunny,
Today you asked me, "What's your favourite thing in the world?"
I like so many things, I decided to write them all down.

I like the mornings, when you wake me up
and help me find my shoes and socks.
You always know which ones are my favourites.

I like breakfast, and so do you!
I think porridge is the yummiest
but you like toast and jam.

You always blow on my porridge so it's not too hot.
That's because you are a very nice bunny.

When we've finished eating,
I like going on the swings.
You never mind that I can
go higher than you.

I will push you and
then you can go high too!

I like when we play together,
kicking leaves, and throwing balls,
and climbing trees!
It's so much fun to play...

But sometimes, I like it when we sit and watch.

I like going to the zoo lots and lots!
But sometimes I get scared of the chimpanzee.

You are the bravest bunny I know,
and when you hold my hand, I feel braver, too.

I like the end of the day,
because then it's bath-time.
We always play splashing!
I always like it, too.

But sometimes I can splash too hard
and then I have to say sorry.

But I like that you're there when I'm sad too.

I think maybe my favourite thing
is when we look at the stars.
Someday we will count them all!

Or maybe my favourite thing is story time.
I like your stories. They are very good
and they give me good dreams.

Dear Bunny,

I've decided I like all the things we do together...

But my favourite thing in the world is YOU!